W9-BLJ-938

4163

WITHDRAWN

The Furry News

How to Make a Newspaper

For Linda

Champion Slug Wins Race

Library of Congress Cataloging-in-Publication Data

Leedy, Loreen.
    The furry news : how to make a newspaper / written and illustrated by
Loreen Leedy.
            p.   cm.
    Summary: Big Bear, Rabbit, and the other animals work hard to write, edit,
and print their newspaper, ''The Furry News.'' Includes tips for making your own
newspaper and defines a number of newspaper terms.
    ISBN 0-8234-0793-4
    2. Newspaper publishing—Juvenile literature. 2. Journalism—Juvenile
literature. [1. Newspapers.] I. Title.
PN4776.L4 1990   89-20094   CIP   AC
070.4—dc20   ISBN 0-8234-1026-9 (pbk.)

The Furry News

How to Make a Newspaper

written and illustrated by
LOREEN LEEDY

Holiday House / New York

One morning, as the animals were eating breakfast,
Big Bear rattled his newspaper impatiently.

Big Bear gave every animal a job.

He asked Rabbit to be the news editor.

The editor had to decide which stories to
put in the newspaper.

Rabbit handed out assignments to the reporters.

The reporters hurried to make phone calls,
ask questions, and take photographs.

Sometimes, it was tough to get information, but the reporters kept working.

Each reporter gathered all the facts,
checked to make sure they were true,
then started writing.

Rabbit read each news article and suggested changes.

Next, Rabbit wrote an exciting headline for each story.

She also wrote an editorial—her opinion about a news story.

Big Bear asked Fox to be the features editor.

The reporters got their assignments from Fox.

They wrote feature articles about movies, television, and books,

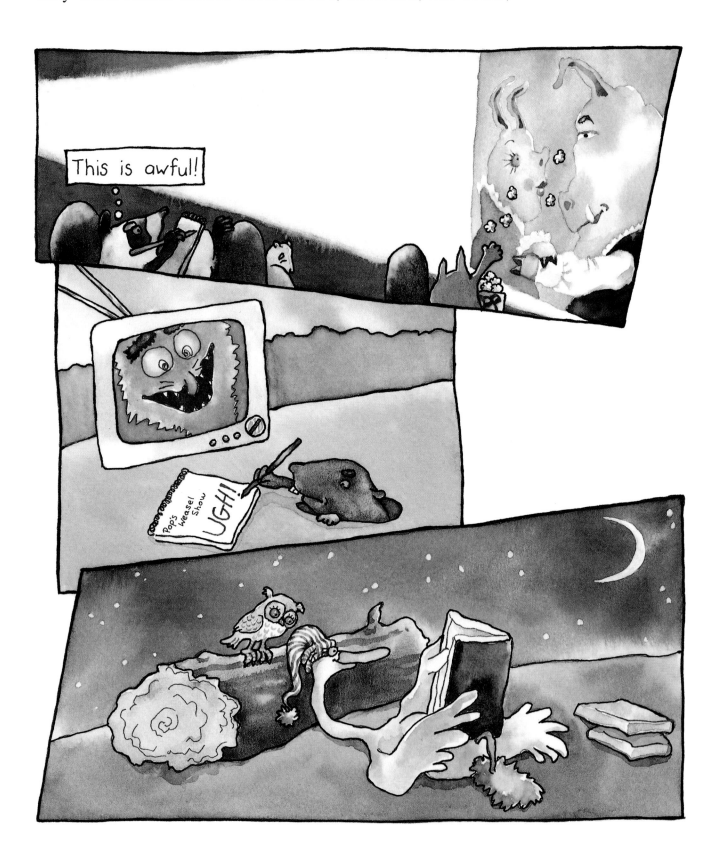

festivals, food, and fashion,

parties, personalities, sports, and whatever else
readers would want to know.

The animals created games and comics for readers to enjoy.

They sold space in the newspaper for advertisements.

The words were set in columns of type and paste-up began.
The news articles, features, and ads fit together like a puzzle.

The newspaper was almost ready to be printed.
The animals checked again for mistakes.
They hurried to finish on time.

The printer made many copies of the newspaper.

They were delivered right away, so everyone could read *The Furry News*.

Making Your Own Newspaper
For Your Family, Neighborhood or School

How To Get Started

Think of a name for your newspaper and decide which stories to include.

Gather the Facts

Interview people who have information. Visit the location where the story is taking place. Search the library for more details.

Write important names, dates, and other facts on paper, and/or use a tape recorder. Take photographs, if possible. (Black and white will reproduce best.)

Check all facts to make sure they are true.

Write the Story

Make an outline or rough draft first. Put the basics of WHO, WHAT, WHERE, WHEN, WHY, and HOW at the beginning.

Check spelling and punctuation, then write the final version.

Write a headline that tells the story in a few words.

Set the Words in Columns

If available, use a computer to prepare and print your newspaper.

Or, use the following materials:
$8\frac{1}{2}'' \times 11''$ typewriter paper
ruler
non-reproducing blue pencil (won't print)
black fine-line marker
typewriter (optional)
scissors
clear tape or glue stick
liquid correction fluid
photocopy machine

Use blue pencil to mark several sheets of $8\frac{1}{2}'' \times 11''$ paper as shown.

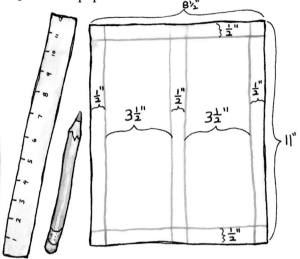

Write out the headline and underline it. (See headlines on these pages.)

Type or neatly handprint story, keeping inside the blue lines.

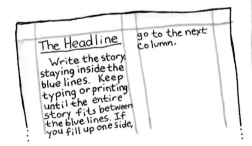

Draw newspaper name in large letters with black marker or use dry transfer letters (available in a stationery store.)

Begin to Paste up Paper

Gather columns, photos, and drawings (drawn with black marker) and arrange them on one or more pieces of blue pencil-lined $8\frac{1}{2}'' \times 11''$ paper. Cut columns apart if necessary.

When everything fits, use glue stick or clear tape to fix in place.

Print Your Newspaper

Make one photocopy. If it looks good, make as many copies as needed.

If dark lines show, use liquid correction fluid to cover. Make photocopies from corrected version.

If your newspaper has two or more pages, use three staples on left edge to hold. Deliver newspapers to readers.

GLOSSARY

ARTICLE: a written report about true events.

CIRCULATION: the process of delivering newspapers to readers; also, the number of newspapers purchased.

COLUMN: a narrow block of type on a page.

DEADLINE: the time when a newspaper must be finished.

EDIT: to read and correct an article for publication.

EDITOR: the person who directs the reporters and decides which stories will be in the newspaper.

EDITORIAL: an article written by an editor that expresses an opinion about the news.

FEATURE: anything in a newspaper that is not news or advertising.

HEADLINE: large type above an article that tells the story in a few words.

INTERVIEW: a conversation in which a reporter seeks information from someone.

JOURNALIST: a person who gathers, edits, and/or writes about the news.

LEAD: the beginning of a news article that includes the important facts.

NEWS: accurate information about important events.

PAPER CARRIER: a person who delivers newspapers.

PAPER ROUTE: the path a paper carrier follows to deliver newspapers to readers.

PASTE UP: to arrange words and pictures on a page before printing.

PUBLISHER: the person in overall charge of a newspaper.

REPORTER: a person who collects information and writes news or feature articles.

SCOOP: a news story that one newspaper publishes first.

TIP: helpful information about a news story given by an outsider.

TYPE: the letters used for printing.